KT-145-096

The Willow Street Kids

Be Smart,
Stay Safe

Michele Elliott is the Director of Kidscape, set up after a very successful pilot study involving thousands of parents, teachers and children being taught 'good sense defence'. A teacher, child education psychologist and mother of two, she has worked with children and adults for twenty-two years.

She is on the advisory councils of the NSPCC and ChildLine and has been awarded a Winston Churchill Fellowship.

Also by Michele Elliott

The Willow Street Kids: Beat the Bullies
Bullying – Wise Guide

The Willow Street Kids

Be Smart,
Stay Safe

Michele Elliott

MACMILLAN CHILDREN'S BOOKS

First published 1986 as *The Willow Street Kids*
by Marilyn Malin Books
Published 1987 by Pan Books Ltd
This edition published 1997 by Macmillan Children's Books
a division of Macmillan Publishers Limited
20 New Wharf Road, London N1 9RR
Basingstoke and Oxford
Associated companies throughout the world
www.panmacmillan.com

ISBN 0 330 35184 2

Copyright © Michele Elliott 1986

The right of Michele Elliott to be identified as the
author of this book has been asserted by her in accordance
with the Copyright, Designs and Patents Act 1988.

All rights reserved. No reproduction, copy or transmission
of this publication may be made without written permission.
No paragraph of this publication may be reproduced, copied or
transmitted save with written permission or in accordance with
the provisions of the Copyright Act 1956 (as amended). Any
person who does any unauthorized act in relation to
this publication may be liable to criminal prosecution
and civil claims for damages.

5 7 9 8 6

A CIP catalogue record for this book is available
from the British Library.

Phototypeset by Intype London Ltd
Printed by Mackays of Chatham plc, Chatham, Kent.

This book is sold subject to the condition that it shall not,
by way of trade or otherwise, be lent, re-sold, hired out,
or otherwise circulated without the publisher's prior consent
in any form of binding or cover other than that in which
it is published and without a similar condition including this

Contents

A Note to Adults

As adults we are all concerned to protect children. The aim of THE WILLOW STREET KIDS is to make them less vulnerable to dangerous conditions. It helps them to think about what to do in many different situations that may confront them.

It is written so that children may read it on their own or so that parents, teachers, grandparents or other adults can read it to or with them. Many junior age children have had or will have experiences with bullies, with flashers or with upsetting telephone calls, all of which are dealt with in the stories. They are a valuable aid in opening up discussions about these situations and what to do, in a non-frightening and practical way, and about the whole area of good and bad touching and other forms of interference.

Children are often warned about the dangers of talking to strangers, and it is important to give them strategies for keeping themselves safe should they be approached by a stranger. It is also essential that children be aware that they should tell and get help if an older person they know tries to touch or kiss them in a secretive way which makes them feel uncomfortable or unsafe. Unfortunately we are finding that many children have to face this possibility and they don't know what to do or how to get help.

The episodes in THE WILLOW STREET KIDS

are true stories told by children themselves. The adults in the book are supportive – they listen to and help the children; though it's made clear that sometimes it's hard to find an adult who will believe you and you must go on trying. The children also help one another. No questions or concerns are left unanswered.

Should children tell you about an incident or problem which has confronted them, listen calmly and be reassuring. The incidents will probably be about bullies or other things that commonly happen. By showing a willingness to listen to these concerns, you will be giving children the message that should anything happen, you will be there to help. This could give children the confidence to tell you if anything else occurs.

What if, for example, someone known to them asked them to keep touching or kissing a secret? Children rarely, if ever, lie about this. Knowing that you will listen, believe and try to help might stop a potentially harmful problem before it starts. That's what this book is about – using children's own stories to help prevent them being harmed. We call it 'good sense defence'.

Michele Elliott

See pages 91 to 96 for where to turn for further help or information.

Introduction

THE WILLOW STREET KIDS stick together and help one another through thick and thin. Some of them have to decide what to do with a very difficult and tricky problem. Their adventures and dilemmas will help you to figure out what to do if any of the things that happen to them ever happens to you or to a friend.

For example, what would you do if someone you know tries to touch or hug or kiss you in a way that makes you feel uncomfortable or unsafe? That person might tell you to keep the touching a secret. THE WILLOW STREET KIDS will help you work out what to do.

The stories in the book are all true and have been told by children whom they have happened to. THE WILLOW STREET KIDS find out what to do when bullies, strangers and even people they know try to harm them. The children also find out who will help them and who their good friends are.

It often helps if you can find an adult you trust to talk to, like your mum, dad or an aunt or uncle. But remember, if you ever need someone to tell and

1

can't find anyone, there *are* people who try to help. Ring any of the numbers in the back of this book on pages 91 and 92. An adult will listen to you and try to help.

CHAPTER ONE

The Bully in the Park

It was the last day of the summer holidays and the Willow Street Kids couldn't believe it was already time to go back to school. It was warm and the sun had shown itself this morning, though the clouds were now looking threatening. But the gang had planned this day out for weeks and a little rain wasn't going to put them off.

We might even be able to find a secret place to hide if it rains, thought Amy, who always looked on the bright side. Short people had to be optimistic. Amy had been the smallest kid in class last year and had spent the entire summer hopefully measuring herself in the mirror. She reckoned she had gained at least a couple of centimetres through all those stretching exercises. Her thick brown hair flew in every direction as she rode her bicycle at top speed.

'I'm going to miss them if I don't hurry. Come on you short old puny legs, go!'

Turning the corner at a hundred kilometres an hour, she was suddenly aware of a figure in front of her. Amy yelled, 'Watch out!!' but it was too late. She rode smack into Charlie.

3

'Watch where you're going, short stuff!' shouted Charlie as he landed in a heap on the pavement.

'Sorry, Charlie,' apologized Amy as she helped him up. 'But if you don't stop calling me that . . .' Amy collapsed in giggles as Charlie formed his face into a mask fit for Halloween.

'By the way, why haven't your freckles grown together yet? Must be an easier way to get a tan!'

Everyone teased Charlie about his freckles, which he hated. He didn't have any choice since his whole family had freckles practically from the moment they were born.

'All right, all right! Truce?'

'Truce!'

'We'd better hurry or the kids will have gone without us.'

'There's no way they'll leave without me,' said Charlie, 'I've got the sandwiches for the picnic. Beat you to the park!'

Amy and Charlie raced breathlessly into the park five minutes later, Charlie winning by a bicycle length.

Gill, Mark, Deirdre, Katie, Tim and Steven were already there, looking impatient.

'About time, too,' scolded Katie. She wrinkled up her nose and shook her head emphatically. She hated anyone to be late.

'As long as you brought the rest of the food,' said Gill. Food was always a problem for Gill, who had a particular fondness for cream cakes. Gill had always been what friends called just nice and plump. With her ginger curly hair and green eyes, she resembled a well-fed tiger cat. But she had worked all summer on not eating so much and felt today she could splurge.

'Come on, let's go and find somewhere to eat,' urged Steven. 'I'm starved!' Steven could eat and eat and never seemed to fill up or out. He just got taller and taller. It didn't help that his afro hair style added even more centimetres. He was the tallest kid in the group.

'Will you stop thinking of your stomach?' retorted Charlie, holding up the bag of food tantalizingly.

'Everyone's here except Julia,' said Tim. He took off his glasses and peered shortsightedly at the sky. 'It's definitely going to rain,' he pronounced. Tim was usually right. He was specially good at science and had a telescope at home to study the sky.

'She probably won't come again,' sighed Deirdre. 'She hasn't done anything with us for the last month.' Deirdre expressed disapproval at yet another delay. 'I don't know why we can never get organized around here.' She was feeling specially grown-up because her older sister had promised to help her plait her hair into braided black locks with little beads attached at the ends, as soon as she had time.

'Let's just wait another minute or two,' pleaded Gill. 'I rang her last night and she said she'd try to be here.'

The children looked at the feast they had brought – sandwiches, crisps, drinks, carrots (from Deirdre's mum, who always included something healthy), cakes, sweets and apples.

'Looks pretty good to me,' said Amy.

After a few minutes, Gill decided Julia wasn't going to arrive after all. 'I s'pose we'd better go,' she said.

They packed up the food and started off to find the best place to put out the picnic.

They rode round and round, rejecting place after place. Finally Mark stopped dead, looked at the rest of the group and declared: 'If we don't find a place soon, we'll have to eat in the rain. Let's stop being so fussy!' Mark liked to make quick decisions. This was driving him mad!

'All right,' declared Deirdre. 'I vote for over there.' She pointed to a spot under two giant trees.

'Great!' shouted Gill and Steven together. They raced to the trees, followed closely by the rest.

They set about putting out the food, which was soon just a happy memory. As they lay around on the grass, they talked about who their new teacher was and wondered about the kids they hadn't seen all summer.

'Do you think Mrs Simpson is as nice as we've heard she is?' wondered Gill.

'My sister had her as a teacher two years ago and she's OK,' replied Steven.

'Maybe she's changed,' said Tim.

'We'll soon find out!'

'I wish we had another week off.'

'I'm *glad* school's starting,' said Katie. Then she suddenly remembered that she had to ring her mum about her appointment with the dentist.

'Back in a minute,' she shouted over her shoulder as she rode off towards the telephones.

Katie was getting out her purse, when an older girl she had never seen before came up to her.

'What are you doing?' said the girl to Katie.

'Ringing home,' replied Katie, starting to enter the telephone box.

'Just wait a minute, I want to talk to you,' the girl said aggressively.

Katie began to feel uncomfortable. Why was this girl talking to her anyway? She hesitated.

'How much money have you got?'

'Only enough for this call,' said Katie.

'You've got lots of money! Let me see your purse.'

The older girl snatched Katie's purse out of her hand and opened it.

'You see? I knew you had more. Now I'm just going to borrow this money.'

The girl threw Katie's purse at her and walked off.

'You can't do that!' said Katie.

'Who's going to stop me?' The girl just laughed.

Katie looked round frantically for someone to help, but there was no one in sight. The girl and her money were gone and she couldn't believe what had happened. She was so angry that tears were streaming down her face as she rode back to the picnic.

'Katie, what's the matter?'

'Some girl just took all my money and ... .' Katie stopped, as the children crowded round asking questions all at once.

'Wait a minute,' said Steven. 'Let's see if we can find her.'

They all rushed to get their bikes and followed Katie to the phone box.

There was no one there.

They rode around for half an hour and had no luck. Tim had just said that it was getting late, and maybe they should ring the police or someone, when Katie pointed excitedly in the direction of the playground.

'Look!' she said in a loud whisper. 'It's her.'

The children hid and watched the older girl. She was eating an ice-cream.

'I bet she bought that with my money.'

'Let's wait until she walks away and then demand Katie's money back.'

'We couldn't, she's bigger than we are. I think we should go for help.'

'Look, she's leaving. Let's follow her.'

The girl was walking out of the park, when she noticed the children. Then she saw Katie and began to run.

'Not so fast, dynamite!' said Steven, pulling up next to her. The children surrounded her with their bicycles.

'Leave me alone. What do you think you're doing!'

'Where's Katie's money?'

'I don't know what you're talking about.'

'Oh, don't you!' said Katie, feeling quite strong with all her friends there.

'You took my money and I want it back.'

The girl looked about her. 'Get out of my way,' she snarled.

'We aren't moving until you give it back.'

'Maybe we should ring the police after all,' said Deirdre.

'The police?' The girl started shaking. 'Look, it was only a joke. I was just borrowing it and I was trying to find you to give it back when you found me.'

The girl handed Katie her money.

'Please don't ring the police. I won't do it again. I'll get beaten if you tell.' She looked quite miserable.

'Rubbish,' said Tim. 'I say we ring the police.'

The girl began to cry. 'Please don't. I won't do it again. I promise.'

Katie looked at the girl and then at the rest of the children.

'What's your name?'

'Judy.'

'All right, Judy, but we're going to keep an eye on you and if you ever do anything like this again, we'll tell.'

Judy looked at her. Then she turned and hurried off, half running.

'I still think we should have rung the police,' said Tim.

'Yes, probably, but I was sorry for her. Did you see that bruise? Maybe she *would* have been beaten,' said Katie.

'It'd serve her right, though,' said Mark.

'Well, but at least I got my money back. Thanks

for helping me,' said Katie. 'I never could have done that on my own.'

'It was nothing,' said Steven.

'What are friends for, anyway?' said Mark.

'It's getting late, and I've got to go to the dentist,' said Katie.

'Are you going to tell your mum what happened?'

'Yes, and my dad. See you tomorrow and thanks again.'

'Bye.'

'Bye, see you.'

Riding home together, Charlie and Amy talked about what happened.

'I think Katie was right to let her go, don't you?' said Charlie.

'Not me. Now Judy will probably go and pick on someone else.'

'I bet she'll stop. She was really scared.'

'Don't count on it.'

They came to the corner where they had collided earlier.

'Anyway, I'm going to get my things ready for school. See you tomorrow.'

'Bye.'

CHAPTER TWO

What Would You Do If . . .

Gill raced into the classroom, dripping with rain. She had run all the way to school.

'Mrs Simpson, Mum said we could have Gus home for the weekend!' she shouted.

'That's wonderful, Gill. Did you bring a note?'

'Right here,' said Gill.

'She'll probably make him into gerbil pie,' said Charlie as he walked in. 'She's always so hungry!'

'Oh, buzz off,' replied Gill.

Tommy laughed. 'I bet she'd fancy some green gerbil jelly.'

Gill indignantly ignored them both.

'Everyone sit down and get out your reading,' called Mrs Simpson. The children had decided that Steven's sister was right. Mrs Simpson was not only nice, but had often talked with them about interesting things besides their school work. And she really seemed to listen to them.

It was still pouring with rain when the break came, so the class had to stay in. Mrs Simpson called them together.

'You can read quietly or paint or play games. If anyone would like to, I'll play *What If* games with you.' Tommy, Steven, Amy, Gill, Katie, Tim and Charlie decided to play. Everyone else found something to do in the room. 'I wish we could go outside in the rain,' said Amy. 'I love getting wet!'

'All right,' said Mrs Simpson, 'I'll start with a pretend situation. What would you do if a giant dragon marched into our classroom?'

'Slay him!' said Charlie.

'Make him a pet,' said Amy, who already had six goldfish, a hamster, a cat and two dogs.

'Not likely,' said Tim.

'Ask him in for tea,' said Katie.

'He wants to have *you* for tea,' said Gill.

'That was a warm-up, but let's try a more serious one. What would you do if you saw thick black smoke coming out of your neighbour's house?'

'Tell my mum.'

'Getting an adult to help is a good idea.'

'Ring the Fire Brigade,' offered Charlie.

'Yes, how would you do that?' asked Mrs Simpson.

'Dial 999,' said everyone together. They had practised making emergency calls before.

'That's right, in Britain,' said Mrs Simpson. 'There's a different number to ring in countries around the world. You need to find that out wherever you are. Does anyone remember what happens when you ring the emergency number?'

'First, the operator says "Emergency, what is your number?" You tell your telephone number.'

'Well done, then what happens?'

Gill continued: 'They ask which service you want, ambulance, police or fire. You say which one and the operator puts you through. Then they ask your telephone number again, and then your name and exactly where you are. Then they send help.'

'Excellent, Gill,' replied Mrs Simpson. 'What else could you do?'

'But what if you didn't have any money and it was a pay phone?' interrupted Charlie.

'You don't need money – just dial 999 and they answer,' said Gill.

'I'd try to put the fire out,' said Katie.

'That would be dangerous! My gran's chip pan caught on fire and she threw water on it and nearly blew up her flat,' said Steven.

'You do have to be careful about how you put out fires and what you use,' agreed Mrs Simpson. 'Some things like water on burning oil make the fire worse. Maybe we should get the fire safety officer to come round and we could ask him about what to do in case of fire. The best idea is to get an adult to put it out.'

'Your gran should have put a wet blanket over the pan. That would have put it out,' said Amy.

'I'd see if anyone was hurt and help them,' said Tim who wanted to be a doctor.

'Help, help Dr Tim!' squealed Charlie, falling on the floor in a heap.

'Oh, leave off, Charlie! I wouldn't help *you*!' said Tim disdainfully.

Ignoring Charlie, Mrs Simpson said, 'It's a good

idea to try to help, but only if it doesn't put you in danger. Remember it's important to keep yourself safe, too.'

'Arghhh! Keep me safe from Dr Tim.' Charlie was getting a bit carried away.

'That's enough, Charlie,' said Mrs Simpson in THAT voice. Charlie sat up, looking sheepish.

'Now it's your turn to make one up,' she said to the children.

'What would you do if someone came up to you and punched you right on the nose?' asked Steven.

'Punch him back,' chorused Tommy and Gill.

'Run away,' said Amy.

'Tell the teacher,' said Katie.

'Let's take the suggestions one at a time,' said Mrs Simpson. 'What would happen if you punched the bully on the nose?'

'You'd get punched back,' said Charlie.

'All right, so you wouldn't solve anything that way. Running away is a good way to keep yourself safe from a dangerous situation. What about telling?'

'Sometimes you need grown-up help,' reasoned Katie, 'especially if you're really in trouble.'

'I agree,' said Mrs Simpson. 'Now, I have another one for you. What would you do if a friend of yours offered you fifty pence to steal something from a shop?'

'Tell them to buzz off,' said Gill, who often said that, especially to the boys.

'Some friend!' remarked Katie.

'Depends on how much I needed fifty pence!' said Charlie.

'How about some serious ideas?' Mrs Simpson was laughing.

'Tell the police,' said Tim.

'Tell my mum,' said Steven.

'That's better! Yes, telling someone you trust when you need help is always a good suggestion.'

'Say no and go away,' said Tommy.

'Standing up for yourself isn't always easy, is it? Saying no to friends is even harder, but that would be the best thing to do. Can anyone tell me what the fifty pence is?'

'Money?' said Charlie.

Mrs Simpson laughed again. 'What is it called when someone offers you money or a present to do something you don't want to do?'

'A bribe,' said Amy.

'That's right,' said Mrs Simpson. 'It's not like a gift, is it? When someone gives you a gift, you don't have to do anything for it. A bribe is used to trick you.'

'Charlie once tricked me into giving him ten pence to see a magic show,' said Tim. 'Some magic! I could see the hole in the table where the rabbit disappeared.'

'Yes, but that's not a bribe,' said Amy. 'Charlie wasn't making you do something you didn't want to do. You wanted to see his show.'

'Not after the first five minutes!'

Charlie shrugged. 'Someday when I'm a famous magician, there'll be queues for my show.'

15

'I'll bet!' said Tim, snorting.

'Never mind,' said Mrs Simpson, 'let's . . .'

'It's stopped raining!' called Sam. 'Can we go out?'

Mrs Simpson looked out of the window. 'You can have ten minutes if you hurry.'

The class quickly got their rubber boots on and rushed out. Mrs Simpson was really glad to be able to sit quietly for a minute. She liked playing *What If* games with the children because it helped them to think about using common sense in keeping safe, helping others and getting help for themselves if they needed it. As she was making up some more questions to ask for the next game, the rain pelted down again and the class rushed in, scattering raindrops everywhere. So much for a peaceful moment!

CHAPTER THREE

The Flasher

'Great goal!' exclaimed the coach to Charlie.

'Thanks, Mr Lockwood,' said Charlie.

It was Saturday morning and the boys had just finished practice.

'Time to change, now. The girls are meeting in fifteen minutes, so make it quick!'

'How did you like that?' grinned Charlie.

'Not bad.'

'What do you mean, not bad? It was stupendous!'

'So you say!'

Charlie was on top of the world. It was his tenth goal this season and he had decided to give up magic in favour of professional football.

He danced around the dressing room.

Charlie was becoming obnoxious lately. Thought he was the star. The boys were fed up.

'Let's get him,' whispered Tommy to Mark. The word went round.

Suddenly six boys appeared out of nowhere and pounced on Charlie.

'Hey, what do you think you're doing,' yelled Charlie.

'Just going to help you have a shower to cool you down a little,' laughed Mark.

'Oh no you don't!' Charlie squirmed to get free, but the boys held on and dragged him towards the shower.

'Nice cold water helps to shrink big heads, Charlie.'

'Try it, you'll like it.'

Charlie pleaded, but to no avail.

'Ahhh,' shouted Charlie, as they ducked his head under. The water was freezing!

He leaped out of the water and chased Tim round the benches.

'Wait till I get my hands on you,' he shouted.

'Try magic,' teased Tim.

'It won't be a spell I cast on you when I get you . . .'

Mr Lockwood walked in just then. 'Hurry up boys, the girls are waiting. Charlie, why did you wash your hair with your clothes on?'

'Just for fun, Mr Lockwood,' said Charlie. He went to get dressed, thinking of how he could change Tim and Mark into toads.

'Come on, Charlie, let's go!' called out Tim.

Mark, Tommy, Steven and Tim were waiting at the door.

'Think you're smart, don't you?' said Charlie.

'Can't take a joke?' replied Tommy.

'Some joke!'

'Look, we didn't hurt you. You only got wet. Don't be such a drip. Ha ha.'

Charlie was quiet as they waited for Tim's dad to pick them up. Actually he was his stepfather, but he had been Tim's dad since Tim could remember.

I suppose I've been getting on people's nerves lately, thought Charlie.

'Let's go to the cinema this afternoon,' suggested Mark.

'Great idea.'

'Yes, let's.'

'How about you, Charlie?'

'Why not?' Charlie grinned.

'I don't think my mum will let me,' said Tommy. 'I'll ring you after lunch.'

As they stood there talking, Tim noticed a man standing not far away. He didn't pay any attention to him.

A few minutes later, Tim saw that he had moved a little closer and was standing quite still. Tim looked at him.

'Look at this, boys,' said the man with a silly smirk on his face.

The boys turned towards him.

The man was standing there with his trousers unzipped, showing his private parts.

'Yuck!'

'Disgusting!'

'I'd put that away, you might catch cold!' shouted out Charlie.

'Quiet, you guys,' hissed Steven. 'Don't talk to him.'

19

Just then Tim's dad drove up. 'Want to meet my dad, mister?'

The man took off faster than a jackal.

The boys were buzzing as they got into the car.

'What was that about?' asked Tim's dad.

'Oh, just some dirty old man getting his kicks out of being undressed,' replied Charlie.

'Are you serious? Which way did he go?'

The boys pointed.

Tim's dad got out of the car and looked in that direction. There was no sign of the man.

'I think we'd better tell Mr Lockwood, Dad,' said Tim.

'Good idea!'

They all went back to the Sports Centre.

'Thanks for telling me,' said Mr Lockwood. 'I'll ring the police and keep an eye out for that man.'

The boys returned to the car.

'I'd love to see Mr Lockwood get that guy,' said Charlie.

The boys laughed.

'Best not to pay any attention to people who do that,' said Steven. 'Talking to them gives them a thrill.'

'Right,' said Tim. 'Well, what should we do about the film?'

Tim's dad said he'd take them to the cinema, if someone else would collect them.

'I think my mum will,' said Steven.

'I'll ring you in a flash,' said Charlie, getting out of the car.

'Ugh! That's a terrible joke, Charlie.'

20

'You're all wet, Charlie!' shouted out Steven.
'Very funny!'
'See you later.'
'Thanks for the ride.'

CHAPTER FOUR

The Right to be Safe

It was the end of another day when Mrs Simpson asked the children to come together at the front of the room.

'Let me ask you a question. What if I told you that no one in the class could eat all day,' she said. 'Would you have problems?'

Gill, who loved biscuits and sweets, laughed and poked Mary. Mary said she would starve.

'I'd go on strike and not come to school,' said Charlie. He was ready to organize the pickets.

'Can anyone tell me another right you have?'

'The right to look at the stars,' said Tim.

'The right to play with my friends,' said Gill.

'I have the right to go to bed later than my little sister,' said Mary.

'Those are all good examples of rights. You have the right to eat, sleep, play and to do most things, as long as you're not hurting someone else and are obeying the law.' Mrs Simpson paused. 'You also have the right to be safe.

'I'm going to tell you a story about a boy who has his right to be safe taken away from him. But first, can you tell me when you feel safe?'

'At home with Mum and Dad,' said Mary.

'With Arnie,' said Charlie.

'Under the covers with my dog,' said Tony.

'Away from my little brother who's a pest,' said Mark.

'I like your brother,' teased Gill, 'he's cute.'

'Yuck!' muttered Mark in disgust.

'In school,' said Laura.

Mrs Simpson continued: 'This story is about a bully who takes something away from a boy called Chris, so let's hear the story and then decide what Chris can do to try to stop the bully and keep himself safe.'

Chris was in the park after school. Mum had told him not to go to the park without his older brother, but Chris got bored waiting for his brother and went. He played for a while on the swings and the roundabout. The slide was broken so he decided to try the climbing-frame. He was about half way up when an older and bigger boy, Oliver, came up to him. Chris knew he was a bit of a bully.

'Come down here for a minute,' said Oliver. 'I want to talk to you.'

'Wait till I get over the top,' said Chris.

'Get down here now or I'll come and get you.' There was something mean in Oliver's voice.

Chris came down.

'What have you got in there?' said Oliver, pointing to the bag Chris had left on the ground.

'Nothing,' replied Chris.

24

'I bet there's something to eat in there. Let's see it. Now.'

Chris reluctantly handed Oliver the bag.

'I was right. Sweets. Now,' said Oliver, 'you meet me here and bring me more sweets. And don't tell anyone, understand?'

Chris nodded.

'Get out of here.'

Chris left and ran home.

'What could Chris do?' asked Mrs Simpson.

'Well, he could tell his mum,' said Laura.

'No way!' said Mark. 'His mum would kill him for going to the park without his brother.'

'He could punch Oliver,' volunteered Steven, catching Katie's eye. They were both thinking of the time last summer when the girl took Katie's money.

'Only if he wanted to be punched back,' said Tommy. 'Oliver is a lot bigger.'

'Call in Arnold Schwarzenegger – he'll get him!' said Charlie.

'You and Arnie!' said Andrew.

'Maybe he could just say no to the bully,' said Mary.

Mrs Simpson asked the children if they thought that they could say No in a really loud voice. 'Yes!' said the class.

'When I count to three, say No,' said Mrs Simpson. 'One, two, three . . .' 'No,' chorused the class, sounding like sick cows.

'You can do better than that. One, two, three . . .'

'NO!!!!!' shouted the children.

Charlie shouted longer than anyone else.

'That was wonderful,' said Mrs Simpson, 'but now let's think about what else Chris could do.'

'I'd be afraid to say no,' said John.

'How about bringing along my dad, he'd sort him out,' said Tony, whose father was huge.

'Maybe a friend or his brother could go to the park with Chris,' said Mary. 'Besides I think he'd have to tell his mum, even if he did break the rules.'

'She'll find out anyway. Mums always do,' said Andrew.

'My mum would kill me,' said Sue.

'Even if you've broken a rule and get into trouble, you should always tell. Your safety is more important than having broken the rule. Also, it seems like a good idea to get someone to go along to say No to the bully. Maybe a friend or relative.

'Raise your hands if you think Chris should tell his mum.'

Most of the class raised their hands.

'But that's telling tales,' said Tony. 'You aren't supposed to tell on other kids.'

'You can tell if they're hurting you,' remarked Andrew.

'That's different from telling tales just to get someone into trouble,' agreed Sue.

'Or running to the teacher because you want to play with something and someone else is using it,' said Mrs Simpson. 'Not that anyone here would ever do that!'

The children laughed.

'But do remember that it's all right to tell an adult if anyone tries to take away your rights or harm you in any way. That isn't telling tales.'

'How did the story end?' asked Laura. Mrs Simpson continued.

Chris told his brother, and made him promise not to tell. But Chris's brother didn't feel right about keeping this secret and told their mum. She *was* annoyed with Chris for going to the park, but more worried that he might have been hurt.

Chris and his brother went to the park several days later and Oliver was there. He came up to Chris and demanded sweets. When Chris and his brother shouted NO, Oliver looked really surprised.

'Give me your sweets,' he said, looking scowling and threatening.

'NO!!!!' shouted Chris and his brother. 'You leave us alone or we're telling.'

'Oh, you're just a couple of creeps. I don't want your sweets.' With that, Oliver went off to find someone else to bully. He wasn't a very happy person and that's part of the reason he bothered other people.

'He was a coward, too,' said Amy. 'Picking on a younger kid probably made him feel big and important.'

'That isn't the way to be important, is it?' agreed Mrs Simpson.

Katie raised her hand. 'Something like that

happened to me this summer.' She told the rest of the class the story, helped by Tim, Steven and Gill.

'Do you think we should have called the police?' asked Katie. 'My mum thought we should, but I didn't want to get that girl into trouble, especially because I thought she might get hit.'

The children argued back and forth.

'It's her own fault if she got into trouble,' said Mark. 'Besides, she was making up the hitting bit to get you to feel sorry for her.'

'Katie got her money back, so I'd just leave it,' said Sue.

'Let's take a vote,' suggested Amy.

It was half and half.

'What do you think, Mrs Simpson?'

'Well, she did steal Katie's money and I suspect that she might have done that before. But I would be worried about the bruise, as well. Maybe telling the police would have helped because they could have found out if she really was being beaten. Also, they might know if she had been stealing before she tried to take Katie's money.

'How many of you have ever had problems with bullies?'

Practically everyone raised their hands.

'Since it's almost time to go home, we'll carry on with this tomorrow.

'Quickly tell me some of the things you remember about your right to be safe. Tommy?'

'We've got the right not to be bullied,' replied Tommy.

'Good. Amy?'

'We have the right to ask for help if we're in danger.'

'Yes. Tim?'

'We should tell if we get into trouble, even if we broke a rule and we're afraid to tell.'

'Excellent. Charlie?'

'We can say no.'

'You certainly can! Remember that you all have the right to be safe and to do anything you need to do to keep safe. Now, it's time to go *quietly* home. See you tomorrow.'

CHAPTER FIVE

Should Secrets Always Be Kept?

The next afternoon at school, Mrs Simpson asked: 'Why do you think the bully in yesterday's story called the boys "creeps"?'

'He was afraid he'd get into trouble,' offered Steven.

'Maybe they *were* creeps,' piped Charlie.

'I still think Chris's brother shouldn't have told when he promised to keep it a secret,' said Emma.

'Should you always keep secrets?' asked Mrs Simpson.

'A promise is a promise,' said Michael solemnly.

'Your friends wouldn't like you if you told,' said Amy.

'But what if you're in a dangerous situation or someone does something which frightens you, but tells you to keep it a secret?' said Mrs Simpson. 'Is it all right to tell the secret then and get help?'

Everyone was quiet for a moment.

Michael agreed that you might have to tell a secret sometimes.

31

'But only if you really need help,' added Tommy, 'or no one would trust you any more.'

'The kinds of secrets that make you feel unsafe or uncomfortable or confused need to be told so that you can get help,' said Mrs Simpson. 'Can anyone think of a bad kind of secret that should be told?'

'When someone tries to take something from you, but threatens to hit you if you tell.'

'That's right. Any others?'

'If a person you don't know offers you a ride,' said Mary.

'Yes, even if they don't tell you to keep it a secret, you should tell someone immediately.'

'Once at the swimming baths, a teenager tried to pull down my swimsuit and then said not to tell,' said Sue.

'What did you do?'

'I told my mum as soon as she came.'

'Good, that's exactly what you should do,' said Mrs Simpson.

'The Pool Manager talked to the boy and his mum, and he apologized. But I felt so awful when it happened I wanted to sink into a hole!'

'That *would* be embarrassing, but it was good not to keep that secret.'

'If you saw a robbery and the robber said not to tell, you should tell your mum and dad and the police,' said Katie.

'Yes, that's very good and helps keep everyone safe.

'What kind of secrets are good to keep? Some families call them surprises, not secrets.'

'A birthday party,' said Amy.

'A present you make for your dad for Christmas,' said Gill.

'Your mum being pregnant,' said Andrew. Everyone in the class knew that Andrew had a baby coming in his family. He wasn't supposed to tell, but he was so excited that he couldn't help it.

'Those are good secrets,' agreed Mrs Simpson. 'Now, it's time to get ready to go home. You can talk about the story of Chris at home over the weekend with your mums and dads, if you like.

'I'd like you to do something else at the weekend. Write about the best good secret or surprise you can think of and about one kind of secret that someone should tell. They can be made-up stories or real ones. Why don't you discuss secrets and surprises with your families? Also, ask what they would do if you got into trouble, but you had broken a rule and were afraid to tell.'

Mark thought he might ask his mum about that when he got home. He had a good idea for the surprise-secret story, but would have to think about what kind of secret to tell.

He walked out with Charlie and Steven, and had a race to the end of the pavement. Mark lost, but pretended not to care.

Gill had collected Gus and was walking along with Mary and Amy talking about being hungry, and how excited she was to be having Gus home. Maybe she could convince her mum and dad to buy her a gerbil of her own. She so wanted a pet.

'I don't see how Chris could have gone to the park alone in that story,' said Amy. 'My mum would kill me if I went to the park alone.'

'I still think that Chris's brother was telling tales,' said Mary. 'I wouldn't tell on my brother.'

'Rubbish,' said Amy, 'you're always telling tales.'

'I'm not!' pouted Mary. 'It's not telling tales if someone is trying to hurt you, anyway. Careful how you hold that cage, Gill. Gus doesn't like being bounced.'

'Oh, he's fine. Don't be so bossy,' retorted Gill.

As they came to Gill's house, she said, 'Well, I wouldn't want to go to the park on my own. Anyway, it's tea-time and I'm starving.' Gill definitely didn't look as if she was starving. 'Gus needs his tea, as well.'

'Bye.'

'See you Monday.'

Gill came in the door and headed straight for the kitchen.

'Mum, look at Gus, isn't he lovely?'

'Charming!' said her mum, grimacing. She wasn't at all keen on animals. 'Just remember that you promised to look after it by yourself and that I don't want to wake up and find it nibbling my toes in the middle of the night.'

'Gus is a him, not an it,' said Gill. 'He wouldn't do that because he doesn't like toes. But watch out for your ears, he loves those! Why don't you just let him have a nibble now?' teased Gill, bringing Gus close to her mum.

'Get lost until tea's ready,' said her mum, laughing, 'and don't bring that little beast back in the kitchen!'

'Shouldn't talk about Helen that way,' replied Gill, referring to her little sister, as she disappeared into her room.

'Cheeky monkey!' her mum shouted after her.

At the dinner table, Gill told about the story of Chris.

'What would you do if I broke a rule and got into trouble like Chris did?' she asked.

'Well, I suppose I would be annoyed that you didn't do as you were told, but your mum and I would both want you to tell us so we could help,' replied her dad. 'I'm glad you're having talks about these things at school.'

'I've got to write two stories this weekend about good secrets and bad secrets. You know what I think would be the best surprise secret in the whole world?'

'What?' said Mum.

'That you were getting me a gerbil for my birthday!'

'Don't hold your breath,' said Mum.

'It will make a good story, anyway!' said Helen.

'How about the kind of secret you should tell?' asked her dad.

'That's more difficult,' replied Gill, thoughtfully. 'Maybe I'll tell about the time I saw one of the bigger girls taking sweets from Mr Norman's shop. I'm not sure yet, though.'

That night before going to bed, Gill asked her dad about getting a pet.

'We'll see,' he said, giving her a goodnight kiss and a hug. It seemed to Gill that every time she wanted something, her parents said, 'We'll see!'

CHAPTER SIX

The Stranger

After school on the Friday when they were walking home, Mark, Charlie and Steven had another race and this time Mark won. Feeling very pleased with himself, Mark said goodbye to his friends and set off for his house.

He was thinking about asking whether *he* could bring Gus home for the weekend, when a man he had never seen before walked up to him.

'Aren't you William Smith?' asked the man.

'No,' said Mark, never having heard of William Smith, though he did know someone named William.

'I must be mistaken, but you certainly look like him. What's your name, then?' asked the man in a very friendly way.

'Oh, no!' thought Mark. P.C. Baker had been to Mrs Simpson's class and shown them a film about strangers. Mark knew that strangers sometimes tried to trick children into going with them, like saying that your mother was sick or that the stranger needed help in finding a lost puppy.

Mark didn't say anything and began walking away.

'Don't be rude. I only want to be friends. My cat

has brand-new baby kittens and I'd like to show them to you.'

Mark loved baby animals more than anything. Certainly more than his brother (but that wasn't hard). He thought for just a moment that maybe he should go, but then he said, 'No thanks,' in a strong loud voice and kept walking.

The stranger started to walk along with him. Mark was beginning to feel frightened. Why wouldn't the man just go away?

'Don't be like that, son,' said the stranger, as he moved closer to Mark.

Mark had learned never to get too close to a stranger, so he began backing away.

Suddenly the stranger grabbed Mark by the arm and started pulling him towards the road. 'You'd better come with me,' he said in a low voice.

Mark felt frozen. He couldn't breathe and his ears were pounding. Then he remembered what he had been taught to do if he was ever in danger and needed to get away fast.

'Yell, and run,' he thought. He willed his mouth to open.

Then he started yelling a deep, loud yell. The man looked startled, but was still holding on to Mark and dragging him away.

Kick! thought Mark, and he kicked the man as hard as he could in the shins. The stranger yelped and let go of Mark's arm. Mark kept yelling and ran away from the man as fast as he could. He never once stopped or looked back until he was hammering on the front door.

'What's all this noise about?' said his mum, who stopped being annoyed the minute she saw Mark's face. 'Mark, are you hurt? What's the matter?'

Mark told her what had happened. Then he started to cry.

Mum put her arms around him and just held him for a few minutes. It felt so safe to be hugged.

Nicky was dancing around the kitchen whining. 'What happened? Why are you crying? WHAT'S THE MATTER!' he screeched in his loudest voice.

Mum was trying to get him to watch television, but he insisted on staying right there. Finally, she put one arm around Nicky and one round Mark. She said to Mark: 'I'm so glad that you're all right. I'm also very proud of the way you remembered what to do.'

Mark began to feel better. He noticed that his mum was shaking a bit. 'Maybe you should sit down, Mum.'

She shook her head.

'I think we'd better ring for the police and then ring Daddy,' she said. 'I'd like him to come home right away.'

It must be really important to have Dad come home, thought Mark. *Hope he won't be mad at me.*

The police arrived before his dad did.

They asked him lots of questions about what the man had said, where it had happened, what time it was and if there was anyone else on the street.

'What did the man look like?' asked the policeman.

'He was about as old as my dad and had brownish colour hair,' said Mark. 'I think he was wearing a suit and a blue shirt.'

'Did he have a beard or moustache?' asked the policewoman.

'No,' said Mark, 'and he actually looked quite nice and neat. You know, not sort of dirty and scruffy or anything like that.'

'People who try to harm children often look quite "normal",' said the policewoman. 'That's why it's a good idea to stay away from anyone you don't know, especially if they try to talk to you or ask you for directions.

'You've been very clever, Mark,' she continued. 'You kept yourself safe and noticed some things that might help us find the man. We want to try to find out where he lives and question him.'

Mark's dad came in just then, looking worried. 'Mark, are you all right?' he asked anxiously. He wasn't angry with Mark, but he was really angry about the stranger. 'If I got my hands on him . . .' said Dad.

'Oh,' said Mark. 'I think he might have had glasses, but I'm not sure. And he had a funny sort of accent, not like someone from round here.'

After more questions, the police were ready to leave.

'Thank you for coming so quickly,' said Mark's mum.

'We're glad you rang us,' said the policeman. 'We

want to catch this man before any children come to harm. We'll notify the school, so the teachers can warn the children. I expect a note will be sent home to all parents, so that everyone will be specially alert.'

'You'll probably hear your teacher talking about it on Monday, Mark, but she won't mention your name, if you don't want her to,' said the policewoman.

'I don't mind,' said Mark.

'Neither do we,' said his parents.

After Nicky had gone to bed, Mark's parents let him stay up and talk.

'How do you feel now, Mark?' asked his dad, giving him a big hug.

'It was quite scary, really,' said Mark. He felt a bit like crying again, but he felt safe with his mum and dad. It was special to have them both to himself and that made him feel good.

'We're so happy that you're safe.' Mark's mum still looked a bit shaken. 'I'm glad you remembered to do what we practised.'

'I think we should teach Nicky, too,' said Mark.

'You're right, Mark,' said his mum. 'He's old enough to learn to stay a good distance from someone he doesn't know and to run and yell if someone tries to harm him.'

Mark laughed. 'We won't have to teach Nicky to yell. He does that enough already.'

'I've been thinking since this happened about grown-ups approaching children,' said Dad. 'There's no reason for an adult to approach a child who is alone. I've never even asked a child for directions,

41

because I would always ask another adult. A good rule would be never to talk to a stranger, especially if you're alone. If you need help from an adult, go into a shop or ask a group of adults, if possible.'

Just then Nicky appeared. 'What's a stranger?' he asked sleepily.

'A stranger is someone you've never met before. Someone who has never been to our house, or who Mummy and Daddy or Mark haven't introduced you to. If someone like that talks to you, he or she is still a stranger, even if they are nice to you.'

'But why shouldn't you go with strangers?' questioned Nicky.

'Although most people are good to children and try to protect them, there are a few people who might try to hurt children. Since we can't tell who these people are, it's better not to go near anyone you don't know. As I said to Mark, if you need help from a grown-up because you're lost, always go to a person like a shop-keeper or a policeman.'

'But what if you've been lost for a long time and there aren't any shops and a stranger offers to help you?'

'In that case you might not have any choice but to let the grown-up help you, but ask him or her to take you to the nearest telephone so you can ring for help. You should always refuse to hold their hand and keep your distance. That way you could get away if you had to. A grown-up who is really trying to help won't force you to hold their hand and wouldn't be angry if you didn't want to. If the grown-up started

to become angry and tried to force you to do something, then you should yell and run. If you have a bad
feeling about something, *you trust that feeling*.

'We'd never be angry with you if you yelled and
ran from a grown-up because you didn't feel safe.'

Mum had Nicky on her lap and he was beginning
to look very tired. Mark was tucked under Dad's arm
and was also looking sleepy.

'Enough of this tonight,' said Dad. 'We're the
luckiest family in the world with our two boys.
Tomorrow we'll go to the park, if the weather is nice.
We can talk again, if you like.' Even though Mark was
getting almost too big to pick up, Dad carried him up
the stairs to bed. Mum brought Nicky, who was asleep
before they got to the top.

After extra hugs and kisses, Mark fell asleep, too.
Later that night Mark woke up feeling a bit scared.
He climbed down into Nicky's bottom bunk bed and
slept there. After all, even a little brother is sometimes
nice to have around. Tonight Nicky's snoring sounded
good to Mark.

CHAPTER SEVEN

Keeping Safe

Mark met Steven and Charlie on the way to school on Monday morning, and told them what had happened.

Charlie didn't even try to make a joke.

'How awful!' said Steven.

'What's awful?' said Amy coming up behind them, walking with Gill and Katie.

Mark told his story again, while Gill and Amy listened in horror.

'What did he look like?' asked Amy.

'Probably all hairy and ugly,' said Charlie.

'No, he was dressed like my dad when he goes to work. You know, a suit and all that. He seemed a nice man, until he grabbed me.'

'You shouldn't have talked to him at all. My mum says to just ignore anyone who comes up to you on the street, if you don't know them,' said Amy.

'Well, I didn't want to be rude,' said Mark. 'But you can bet, if anyone tries to talk to me again, I'll just walk right by and pretend I don't hear.'

'My mum tells me that I've got to be polite to adults and say hello when they talk to me,' Steven said.

'But not to someone you don't know and haven't met before!' exclaimed Amy.

'But sometimes it's hard to know what to do. My mum says that it's my body and I have the right to say what happens to me and who I should talk to and kiss and all that. Then when my great-aunt leaves, she makes me kiss her goodbye even if I don't want to,' said Katie.

'I think you should tell your mum how you feel,' said Amy.

'My dad told me that it's even all right to be rude to an adult, but only if the adult is doing something that makes me feel unsafe. He said he would never be cross with me if I accidentally hurt someone's feelings if I was frightened,' said Charlie.

'Most grown-ups are really nice, though,' said Steven.

They kept talking till they got to school. By the time the bell rang, all the children knew what had happened to Mark. Everyone was buzzing as they entered the class. Mrs Simpson called Mark aside and asked him how he was feeling.

'Fine, Mrs Simpson, but I didn't sleep very well last night.'

'I bet you didn't,' she said, giving him a hug. 'I'm so glad you're all right. Do you mind being in the class when I talk about what happened?'

Mark said he didn't mind and besides the class already knew that it was him the stranger had tried to grab.

When everyone was sitting down, Mrs Simpson began:

'Something has happened that we all need to know about,' she said.

'Someone tried to kidnap Mark!' shouted out Charlie.

'Oh, be quiet, Charlie,' said Mary.

With Mark's help, Mrs Simpson explained what had happened.

'Let's go over the things to remember should any of you ever be in that situation,' she said. 'Who can think of one of the rules we learned?'

'Never talk to strangers,' said Katie.

'Stay far away from someone you don't know,' said Tim.

'Don't take sweets from a stranger,' said Gill.

'Maybe you could if they were wrapped,' said Tony.

'No,' shouted several of the children, and the rest agreed.

'Just kidding!' said Tony.

'It's all right to yell, kick and run, if you're in danger,' said Charlie.

'If you're in danger and need to get away fast, where should you kick the attacker?' asked Mrs Simpson.

'Where it really hurts!' exclaimed Steven.

The children giggled.

'If you ever try to kick up at an adult, what do you think the adult would do?'

'Grab your leg and push you down,' said Andrew.

47

'That's right. Where is the safest and best place to aim the kick?'

'At the shins, so no one can grab your leg!'

'Good! Can everyone show me where your shins are? Yes, that's right, the bone joined right on to your ankle.'

'Kick the attacker in the shins and run away to get help,' said Sam.

'What if someone puts a hand over your mouth to keep you quiet?'

'Lick it!' offered Charlie.

'Oh, yuck!' said Gill.

'Bite it!'

'Take his little finger, pull it hard back away from your mouth and then yell!' said Tim.

'You can do any of those things. Pulling back the little finger works particularly well. Now let's practise the yell we learned that Mark used,' said Mrs Simpson. 'Everyone stand up. Remember that if you're frightened a yell sometimes sticks in your throat, but not if it comes from your stomach. Stand up, please. When I count three, take a deep breath and let the yell come from right down in your stomach.

'One, two, three . . .'

The children shouted.

'Well done!' said Mrs Simpson. 'You've remembered all the things we practised.

'Today I'll be giving you a note to take home about the stranger who approached Mark and it's very important that you give it to your parents and talk to them about what happened.'

'Wait till the next time my brother tries to get me,' laughed Steven.

'I know you're joking,' said Mrs Simpson, hearing that, 'but everyone must please remember *never* to use any of the ways to protect yourself we've learned in play, or on other people unless you feel unsafe, because you could hurt them. Do you all agree with that?'

'Yes!'

Mrs Simpson then asked if anyone else had ever had something frightening happen to them that they would like to talk about.

'We got some of those awful telephone calls,' said Anne. 'You know, when the person on the other ends says really rude things.'

'What could you do if that happened to you?' Mrs Simpson asked the class.

'My mum told us not to say anything, just hang up,' said Anne. 'But the calls kept coming, so she bought a really loud whistle and blew it down the phone. That stopped them!'

The class laughed. 'Good thinking,' said Katie.

'If the calls don't stop, you should ring the police and they'll investigate,' commented Mrs Simpson.

'We had a flasher at the Sports Centre last month,' said Steven.

The children giggled nervously.

'That can be very frightening,' said Mrs Simpson.

'What are flashers?' whispered Laura to Amy.

'People who show you their private parts,' whispered Amy. 'Like in a park or somewhere on the street.'

What a stupid thing to do, thought Laura.

'What's the best thing to do if that ever happens to you?' asked Mrs Simpson.

'The best thing to do is to turn away and not to say *anything*,' replied Steven. 'Don't talk at all!'

'Yes, and get away from him, if you're frightened.'

'That happened to my friend at a bus stop,' said Anne. 'She just didn't know what to do. No one else seemed to pay any attention.'

'It isn't very pleasant when that happens, but do tell an adult as soon as possible and always remember to ignore the person who is doing it. He wants you to giggle or react in some way and if you don't, it might make him stop bothering you. Anyone else had anything scary happen?'

The children looked around. Everyone was quiet.

'Let's remember that sometimes being scared feels sort of safe, like telling ghost stories with friends or family. But most of the time, being frightened isn't very nice. Who can you tell if you're frightened of something?'

'Grandma.'

'Mum.'

'My dog.'

'My uncle.'

'A friend.'

'My diary.'

'Dad.'

'The police.'

'Even you!'

'Even me?' Mrs Simpson laughed. 'Of course you can tell me. I hope you all know that.'

CHAPTER EIGHT

Dealing With Fears

It wasn't long after they'd had the talk at school when the telephone rang while Deirdre was at home alone. She picked the phone up and said, '223581'.

'Is your mum home?' said a voice.

'Not at the moment. Can I take a message?'

'No thank you, but let me talk to your dad and I'll tell him.'

'Sorry, he's not here either.'

'Perhaps I can tell you. What's your name?'

'Deirdre.'

'Well, Deirdre, what colour are your knickers?'

Deirdre froze as the caller suddenly started saying the rudest things she had ever heard. She slammed down the phone and ran from the room.

About three minutes later she heard the telephone ringing. Maybe it was her mum. She gingerly picked it up.

'Is that 223581?' asked the same voice.

Oh, no, thought Deirdre, *whoever it is knows my number.*

'I can see you,' began the voice, 'don't hang up or I'll come over and . . .' Again the rude words started.

Deirdre tried to remember all those things they

had talked about in Mrs Simpson's class. She put the receiver down and waited for just a second before picking it up again to dial for help. She tried her mum's office. The number was busy.

Where's Sally? she thought. Sally was Deirdre's older sister who was usually home when she got back after school.

The phone rang again. This time she didn't answer it. The ringing went on and on.

I should have left the receiver off, thought Deirdre. She was getting worried. What if the caller really could see her? She closed the curtains and went to check to see if the door was locked.

The phone stopped ringing, just as the front door opened. Deirdre jumped and gave a startled cry.

In walked Sally and her boyfriend with a bag of shopping.

'Hi, we've just been . . .' Sally stopped when she saw the look on Deirdre's face. 'What's the matter?'

'Sally, I'm so glad you're home!' cried Deirdre, hugging her. The words rushed out as Deirdre explained what had happened. Sally and John looked angry.

'Deirdre, are you all right?' asked John.

'I think so,' replied Deirdre.

Just then the phone rang again.

Sally picked it up, listened for a moment and immediately hung up.

'We'll ring for the police,' she said, picking up the phone and dialling. 'It's the caller again. What these people want is for us to react to what's being said.

That's what gives them a thrill. The best thing to do is to say nothing and hang up immediately. Since this man keeps ringing back, we'd better call the police.'

Sally left the receiver off while waiting for the police to arrive. When they came, they took down all the details and promised to try to help.

'The trouble is that these people are difficult to catch. If he does keep ringing, though, we'll arrange for your calls to be intercepted. I suspect he'll stop ringing here when he doesn't get a reaction. Please let us know if it continues.'

No more calls came until later that evening. But this time they were ready.

Deirdre had remembered the whistle trick that Anne had talked about. John went out and bought a shrill whistle and, after making sure it was the obscene caller, blew it into the receiver. That was the last time he rang them!

Deirdre didn't think about the phone calls much after that. She had a busy weekend. Sunday night before she went to sleep, the phone had rung again, but it was only Katie wanting to chat. Katie always left everything until the last minute, even though she hated anyone else to be late.

That night Deirdre was having difficulty getting to sleep. She tossed and turned and when she finally did fall asleep, she dreamed a monster was after her.

'Help! The monster's chasing me!'

'Wake up, Deirdre, it's all right.'

'Oh, Mum, it was after me.'

'Shhh, you'll wake up everyone. There's no monster. You're safe in your own bed.'

'I'm scared!'

'Let's turn on the light for a minute and you'll see that there isn't anything here. Anyway, there are no such things as monsters.'

Her mother could still remember some dreams she'd had when she was younger and how real they had seemed. So she helped Deirdre look under the bed and in the wardrobe and behind the curtains.

'There, Deirdre,' she said, giving her a hug and tucking her back into bed. 'Can you sleep now?'

Deirdre nodded and closed her eyes.

The next morning, walking to school, she remembered how scared she had been and thought how silly it seemed in the daylight. But sometimes at night it was easy to imagine things.

Besides, now that she was getting older, she didn't have bad dreams very often. Mum had said maybe it was because of those phone calls. Deirdre wondered if anyone else at school ever had bad dreams, but she didn't want to ask.

'Hello,' said a voice behind her. It was Katie.

'Hi, Katie,' replied Deirdre. They walked along together, talking.

Deirdre told Katie about the telephone calls.

'Yuck!' said Katie. 'I hope that never happens to me.'

'Sally says the best thing to do is to ignore what the person is saying and hang up right away. If you say anything, it just makes them happy and gives them a thrill. I'll never again give our number, though, when I answer the phone.'

'Why ever not?'

'Well, when you give your number, that person can keep ringing back. Probably our number was just dialled without their knowing who it was, but telling the caller the number made it easy to ring back.'

'I suppose it's not a good idea to say your name, either?' asked Katie. 'I always say our number and then my name. I think I'll talk to my mum and see what she says.'

They talked for a while about other things. Katie had watched the horror film on TV last night.

'My mum said it would be too scary for me,' said Deirdre. 'Was it good?'

'Great,' said Katie, 'but I couldn't get to sleep for a bit!'

'Katie, do you ever . . .' began Deirdre. But Katie interrupted.

'You know,' said Katie, 'once I saw a film about space creatures and I woke up screaming that they were in my room. My brother was just a baby then and he began crying and pretty soon everyone was up. My dad was ready to kill me. I really had to persuade him to let me see that film last night.'

Deirdre told Katie about her dream and was just finishing as they got to school.

'But please don't tell anyone, Katie. I don't want to talk about the phone calls or my dream just yet, all right?'

'Yes, OK,' said Katie.

As they went in, Deirdre was feeling better. She wasn't the only one who got frightened sometimes.

Mark and Tim were there already. They had also seen last night's film.

'I thought it was stupid!' said Mark. 'It wasn't nearly as good as that giant spider film.'

'I hate scary films,' said Andrew, who had just arrived.

'I don't mind them, but I don't like it if it really happens,' said Mark.

They were all quiet for a minute, remembering how frightened Mark must have been that time with the stranger.

'I got lost in a shop once when I was little. I've never been so scared in all my life,' said Tim.

'That happened to me at the zoo a couple of years ago. I still remember the feeling – it was awful,' agreed Gill.

'I think being lost is the most scary thing that has ever happened to me, too,' offered Charlie.

'You should have been there when this man tried to get into the house last year when I was home alone,' said Amy. 'He came to the door while Mum was out shopping. He was dressed in a suit and had a briefcase.'

Everyone stopped talking and listened.

'I didn't open the door, but I thought it might be Mum, so I asked who it was through the door. He said he was a friend of my father's and asked if either my mum or dad was home.'

'You didn't tell him did you?' asked Mary.

'Well, he looked really nice and I thought he might be a friend of my dad's and I didn't want to be rude. I said they weren't home.'

'That wasn't a very smart thing to do,' said Tim. 'You're never supposed to tell anyone if you're home alone.'

'I know, but he seemed so friendly. Anyway, he kept asking to come in and I started feeling that something was wrong. My dad had never sent anyone to the house before. I began to get frightened.'

'What did you do?'

'I told him that I'd just ring my dad and be right back. When I telephoned my dad he said he hadn't sent anyone to the house and he told me not to open the door and to stay on the phone. He got someone else to telephone for the police and he came home right away. The man had gone.'

'You did exactly the right thing,' said Mrs Simpson, who had come to find out why the children weren't in class when the bell rang. No one had heard her come up. 'You must have been feeling quite frightened, Amy.'

Amy nodded. 'I was more scared after it happened. I was glad when my parents came home, I can tell you!'

'*Everyone* gets frightened, at least once in a while. Sometimes feeling scared even helps keep us safe because we know we have to get away or get help, if we're scared.'

'Like Mark did when the stranger tried to grab him,' added Tim.

'Yes, that's right,' said Mrs Simpson. 'Let's all go inside and later today perhaps you can use some of your experiences and feelings when writing in your journals. If anyone wants to talk about this with me, please tell me and we'll find a time to meet.'

The children followed Mrs Simpson into the classroom. There was a lot to think about these days in learning to keep safe!

CHAPTER NINE

Good Touches, Bad Touches

Several weeks later, as the children were coming into the classroom, Julia cried out, 'Look! Gus is sick!'

The class came running. There was Gus, the gerbil, looking quite poorly. He didn't even twitch his whiskers.

'He's breathing,' offered Steven.

'I told you not to handle him so roughly,' said Mary crossly to Gill.

'I didn't!' protested Gill. She looked ready to cry.

Mrs Simpson intervened. 'Let's just leave Gus alone for a while. He's probably having a nap. I'm sure he'll be all right.'

'But Gill shouldn't have . . .' began Mary.

'That's not fair!' Gill interrupted. 'It's not my fault if Gus is sick.'

'All right, that's enough,' said Mrs Simpson. 'Everyone sit down.

'Remember when we got Gus and we talked about the way to feed and hold him?' asked Mrs Simpson.

The children nodded.

'What kind of touches do you think Gus likes?'

'Soft pats,' said Peter.

'Being patted behind his ears,' volunteered Amy.

'Let's think about the kind of touches we like,' said Mrs Simpson.

'I like to be petted behind the ears,' joked Charlie.

'Well, you do look a bit like Gus, Charlie,' said Tommy, quick as a flash.

'I love it when my grandma and grandpa come to visit and Grandpa gives me piggyback rides,' said Mary.

'He must be strong to lift you,' teased Mark.

'I love being tickled,' said Deirdre.

'Not me,' said Sam. 'My cousin tickles too hard and I don't like it.'

'Why don't you tell your cousin to stop?' said Mrs Simpson.

'I do, but she doesn't listen. I suppose she thinks I like it. Besides, she's a lot older than me.'

'Grown-ups don't listen to you, anyway,' said Julia quietly.

'They should,' said Mrs Simpson.

'My dad gives me great big bear hugs,' said Gill, 'and I love them.'

'How many of you like those hugs and kisses from Mums and Dads?' asked Mrs Simpson.

The children laughed and raised their hands, except Charlie who declared himself too old for kisses. He didn't mind hugs, though.

Mrs Simpson said her mother and father still kissed and hugged her. 'I like it, too.'

'Well,' said Charlie, 'my sister likes kisses from her boyfriend.'

'That's different 'cause they're the same age and in love,' said Mary.

'I wouldn't like it!' declared Charlie.

'I like the feeling of having my hair cut,' said Mark.

'Not me!' said George.

'I love it when the sun feels warm on my face,' said Deirdre.

'Yes,' agreed Robert, 'or running your hand through the water.'

'I don't like it when a spider crawls on me!' shuddered Gill.

Several of the children squirmed at the thought.

'We've got a friend who has a beard and I can't stand it when I have to kiss him,' said Katie. 'But Mum and Dad always say I have to because he's old and it might hurt his feelings.'

'How does that make you feel?' questioned Mrs Simpson.

'Sort of guilty because he *is* nice, but angry because I don't want to do it,' replied Katie.

'Do you remember when we talked about rights?' asked Mrs Simpson. 'You have the right not to have to kiss anyone if you don't want to, Katie.'

'But don't you have to do what grown-ups tell you?' asked Julia.

'Adults must listen to children, too. If you're uncomfortable or confused or don't like the way someone is touching you or kissing you, you have the right to say No. Also, no one older than you should ever ask you to keep a kiss, a hug or a touch a secret. If they do, you should tell.'

'What do you mean, someone touching you?' said Steven.

'Most adults want to protect children and would never do anything which would make you feel unsafe. But there are some grown-ups with serious problems who might try to touch you, maybe even in the private parts of your body. Those are the parts of your body covered by your swimsuit.'

The children giggled and looked round at one another.

'Boys sometimes think this only happens to girls, but we know it happens to both boys and girls.'

Mrs Simpson continued, 'This will probably never happen to you, but we need to talk about it so you know what to do just in case someone ever tries. It's like learning how to cross the road or how to get out of a fire, though you may never be in an accident or a fire.

'What could you do if it ever happened to you?' asked Mrs Simpson.

'Say No!' said Charlie.

'But it's hard to say no to a grown-up you know,' said Julia.

'Yes, it is,' agreed Mrs Simpson, 'but it's your body and you have the right to say No. What else could you do?'

'Get away,' said Deirdre.

'Yes, getting away to a safe place is a good idea.

Even if you know the person, you have the right to get away if your safety is threatened. You could leave the room or go to a friend's house or go home. What else?'

'Tell someone,' said Gill.

'That's right.'

'But what if they don't believe you?' asked Julia.

'When that happens, it's not easy, but you should keep telling until someone does believe you and helps you,' said Mrs Simpson. 'Even if something like this has happened to you before and you have never told anyone, telling now is a good idea.'

'What if you have no one in the whole world that you can trust?' asked Steven.

'Then you can ring up one of the organizations that help children and talk to someone over the phone to get advice. I'll put some telephone numbers on the board later for everyone to copy down.'

'But won't the adult get into trouble if you tell?' asked Julia.

'Adults who do this have problems. It's like a sickness. They are already in trouble and need help. The only way to stop this happening is to tell. Besides, telling might prevent it from happening to another child.

'Now, remember we were talking about Gus? He has feelings just like you do. Sometimes he likes to be held and patted and sometimes he wants to be left alone.

'If you don't feel safe, or don't like the way someone is touching you, you should always tell a grown-up. No one should force you to hug or kiss anyone.

'So, what are the things to do if anything like this ever happens to you?' Mrs Simpson wrote on the board.

SAY NO!
GET AWAY TO A SAFE PLACE!
TELL AN ADULT YOU TRUST!
IF THE FIRST PERSON YOU TELL DOESN'T
BELIEVE YOU, KEEP ON TELLING UNTIL
SOMEONE DOES, AND HELPS.

Then she wrote down some of the numbers to ring and got everyone to copy them.*

'Tonight I'd like you all to think of who you would tell if you ever had a problem with someone older than you, and they were trying to touch or kiss you in a way which made you uncomfortable. You don't have to write it down or even share it with anyone, unless you want to. If anyone needs help thinking of people to talk to, either ask your mum and dad or another grown-up. I'll be glad to help, as well.'

Just as Mrs Simpson finished talking, the children heard the wheel go round in Gus's cage.

'He's not sick! He was just sleepy,' laughed Charlie.

'Told you!' said Gill to Mary.

* See pages 91 and 92 for help numbers

CHAPTER TEN

Should I Tell?

The class had a break in the afternoon and went outside.

Amy found Gill on the other side of the playground. They were talking when they noticed Julia. Julia was one of the brightest in the class, but lately she seemed to be upset about something.

'I wonder what's the matter with Julia,' whispered Amy to Gill.

'Don't know, should we go over and talk to her?' whispered Gill back.

'Yes, all right,' said Amy. 'Maybe we can find out why she's always looking so sad lately. I wouldn't be sad if I was first in maths like Julia,' she added.

Gill and Amy walked up to Julia.

'Hi, Julia, what are you doing?'

'Oh, hello. Nothing much,' replied Julia.

'I've been wondering how Mark is now, after that stranger thing. Do you think he's still worried?' asked Amy.

'He must have been really scared when it happened,' replied Julia thoughtfully.

'I'd die if anyone came up and grabbed me,' said Amy.

'Not me,' said Gill, 'I'd do just what Mark did and get away fast.'

'Sometimes it's not easy,' Julia said slowly.

'What do you mean?' asked Gill.

'Well, what if you knew the person who was trying to do something to you? Then you couldn't yell and run,' said Julia.

'No one I know would try to grab me,' said Gill.

'I don't mean grabbing you, I mean maybe trying to touch you or kiss you when you don't want them to,' said Julia.

Gill and Amy looked at each other and then at Julia.

'I still don't understand what you mean,' said Gill.

'Never mind,' said Julia, 'forget I said anything.'

'What's the matter, Julia?' asked Gill.

'Nothing.'

'Come on, you can tell us,' said Amy.

Julia hesitated.

'Let's go over in the corner and be by ourselves,' said Gill.

When they were alone, Amy said, 'Please tell us, Julia. We'll help. Won't we, Gill?'

Gill nodded.

'Well,' said Julia, 'I'll tell you if you promise to keep it a secret. You see, this happened to a friend of mine and she'll get into real trouble if you tell.'

'We promise,' chorused Amy and Gill.

Julia thought for a long time.

'This friend of mine who's our age has this uncle who she's always liked. When she was little he used to be really sweet to her and told her that she was his special girl.' Julia stopped.

'Well, last year he started touching and kissing her, but not in a nice, cuddly way,' said Julia.

'What do you mean?' asked Gill.

'You know what Mrs Simpson was talking about today?' Julia hesitated again.

'You mean he was touching her . . . where he shouldn't?' said Gill quietly.

Julia nodded.

'Why would her own uncle do that?' exclaimed Amy.

'I don't know, but it frightens her,' said Julia.

'She should tell her mum,' said Gill. 'Why doesn't your friend tell?'

'Her uncle said it had to be a secret or she would get into trouble and so would he. She's all confused and doesn't know what to do.'

'Why should she have to keep kisses a secret? You mean she can't tell her mum?' asked Amy.

'Her uncle said if she told her mum, he would say she was lying,' said Julia. 'She's scared her mum won't believe her.'

'Maybe she should tell someone else,' said Gill.

'Like who?' asked Julia.

'Well, she's told you, maybe you could tell your mum and get her help,' said Gill.

Julia got very quiet.

'Or maybe she could tell a teacher or an aunt or someone,' said Gill. 'Maybe you could help her.

Remember what Mrs Simpson said about secrets? This sounds like a secret we shouldn't keep.'

'You promised!' cried Julia.

'All right, all right. Don't panic,' said Gill.

Just then the bell rang to go in.

'Remember, you promised!' said Julia as they walked into the class.

Amy and Gill were still talking about Julia as they walked home after school that afternoon.

'What do you think we should do about Julia's secret?' said Gill.

'Nothing, we promised not to tell and she'll get furious with us if we do,' said Amy.

'But Julia's friend is in trouble and she's frightened. She's got no one to protect her. Oh, I wish I knew what to do,' said Gill.

'Well, I'm not doing anything,' said Amy as they came to her house. 'See you tomorrow!'

Gill went in to have tea, but she hardly ate anything.

'What's the matter, Gill?' asked her mum.

'Nothing.'

'Must be something the matter when you don't eat. Are you ill?'

'No, I think I'll just go to my room for a while.'

Gill thought and thought. She felt she had to do something to help, but what? Maybe she should talk to her mum, without telling her who had the problem. Better still, maybe she could get Julia to tell her own mum and get help for her friend. Or maybe Julia could tell some other adult she could trust.

Suddenly Gill had another thought, one which worried her.

Maybe it's not Julia's friend. Is it Julia that this is happening to and she's too scared to tell? That's why she'd be so upset.

Gill didn't sleep much that night. She decided she had to talk to Julia again.

Next morning, Gill went over to Julia. When they were alone, Gill said:

'Julia, I've been thinking about what you told us and I think we need an adult to help.'

Julia started to shake her head, but Gill went on: 'I've been wondering about this all night and you know what I think?'

'What?' said Julia.

'I think that maybe this uncle might be your uncle.'

'No,' protested Julia, 'don't say that! It isn't true. I made the whole thing up. Just forget it!' Julia ran to the loo, leaving Gill standing there.

Maybe I was wrong, thought Gill. But the more she thought, the more she still believed that her feelings were right. She knew that this was not something she could keep secret. It was a bad secret and someone needed help. She wasn't sure if that someone was Julia, but she was sure that she should tell an adult and get help.

Gill decided she would think about it for one more day and then tell her mum.

CHAPTER ELEVEN

Julia's Bad Secret

That afternoon as Julia waited to be collected, she was worried. Her aunt was picking her up because her mum had taken her sister Tracy to the dentist. She didn't want to go in case her uncle came home. She had pleaded with her mum to be allowed to go along with her and Tracy, but her mum had said not to be so silly.

Besides that, Julia knew she shouldn't have said anything to Gill, because now Gill had guessed her secret and she was afraid that she would get into trouble if Gill told anyone.

Maybe I should try to tell someone, thought Julia, *but who would believe me? I tried to tell Tracy, but she said it was a terrible thing to say and that they would lock me up if I said such things*. Julia was so lost in thought that she didn't see her aunt drive up.

'Julia!' called her aunt. 'Come on, we've got to collect Ben as well.'

Ben, who was two years older than Julia, was her only cousin and she thought he was wonderful. At least he was nice to her, though he wasn't to everyone. He and Tracy didn't get on. He also had some problems at school, but Julia wasn't sure what they were.

'Had a good day at school?' asked Aunt Barbara.

'All right,' said Julia.

They drove in silence and Julia thought some more. *I wonder if Ben could stop his dad doing this? But Ben doesn't get on with him very well and how could I ever tell him, anyway?*

Her thoughts were interrupted by Ben getting into the car.

'Hi, Twink,' he said.

Julia grinned at his nickname for her and they talked all the way to his house. As they were going in, Julia asked, 'Is Uncle Simon home?'

'No, he's working late tonight, so you probably won't see him before your mum comes to collect you,' said Aunt Barbara.

Julia was relieved and went to play video games with Ben. Julia had a great time and even won, sometimes. She decided that Ben was her best friend, even if he was a boy.

'Hello, there, children,' said Uncle Simon. Julia jumped a mile.

'Oh, hello, Uncle Simon,' she said, looking down.

'Hello,' said Ben. 'Mum said you'd be late tonight.'

'Finished earlier than I expected. I'll be back in a minute to see how you're getting on.'

Julia noticed that Ben had gone quiet as well. The lovely time they were having had disappeared. Ben and Julia looked at each other.

Julia started to shake and the words came tumbling out in a whisper. 'Ben, what would you do if a grown-up tried to touch you and you didn't want him to?'

Ben looked at her in amazement. 'Oh, Twink, he hasn't tried it with you, too, has he?'

Julia nodded miserably and then stared at Ben. Had she heard him properly? 'You too,' he had said.

'Ben, you mean Uncle Simon has been touching you . . .' Ben didn't let her finish.

His eyes began to water and he said gruffly, 'Don't you worry about it and don't say a word to anyone. Do you hear? Not anyone!'

Before she could say anything more she heard her mother's car drive up.

'I've got to go, Ben.' She took his hand and squeezed it, but he just sat there without saying anything.

'Hurry up, Julia,' yelled Tracy, 'I've got homework to do and Jenny's coming over.'

'Bye, Ben.'

'Bye, Julia.'

On the way home, Julia said nothing. Tracy chattered on and on about school and how she was going to spend the weekend at Jenny's.

When they got in, Julia's mum said, 'What's the matter, Julia? Didn't you have a good time at Ben's?'

'It was all right,' said Julia, 'but I don't feel very well. I think I'll go to my room.'

'I hope you're feeling better this weekend, Julia,' said her mum. 'Uncle Simon said he would take you and Ben to the fun fair and that you can stay the night. Would you like that?'

Julia felt like screaming 'NO'. Instead she started towards the door. As she turned to go, she said, 'Mum?'

'Just a minute, Julia, there's the phone.'

Julia went up to her room. *I can't tell*, she thought. *But I'm not going over there this weekend or ever again.*

She heard a knock on the door.

'Julia, I want to talk to you. May I come in?'

Her mum came in and sat on the bed.

'What is it, Julia? What's been the matter with you lately?'

Julia felt her heart thumping. She had to try to get help, but did she dare tell?

'You can tell me, Julia. Just take a deep breath and start.'

Julia burst into tears. 'Oh, Mum, I've got this really bad secret and . . .'

CHAPTER TWELVE

The Secret is Out

Just then Tracy came in. Julia fled to the bathroom and locked the door.

I can't tell, she said to herself. *Tracy is right, Mum will be angry with me.*

'Julia?' said a voice through the door. Her mum knocked and called her name louder. 'Julia, come out and we'll have a talk with just the two of us. It can't be that bad.'

'Please go away,' said Julia.

'Only if you promise to talk when you come out,' said her mum.

'I'll be out in a few minutes. Just let me be alone for a little while.'

'All right, take your time.'

Julia went back into her bedroom and closed the door. Tracy wasn't there. She wondered if Tracy had said anything to Mum.

She walked round and round the floor, thinking about what to do.

What if she doesn't believe me? Who could I tell then? Maybe I could talk to Gill's mum or even Mrs Simpson. But grown-ups don't usually believe kids anyway. Maybe I shouldn't say anything. Ben said not to tell. Maybe he's right. Julia threw herself down on her bed and started to cry.

What will happen to Ben and Uncle Simon if I tell? But I can't keep it a secret any more. I don't want to go over there this weekend. I know he'll do it again . . .

Julia sat up straight.

He hasn't got the right to touch my body! she thought, getting angry. *I'm going to tell.*

Julia came into the kitchen. Her mum got up from the table and went over to her, putting her arm round Julia's shoulders.

'Let's go somewhere private and talk,' she suggested.

They were back in Julia's room. Her mum waited.

'Uncle Simon has been asking me to do things . . .' began Julia. She was afraid to say too much in case her mum got angry with her.

'What kind of things?' said her mum, looking very serious.

'Well, he's been asking me to kiss him and . . .' she stopped.

'Yes?' said her mum quietly.

'And . . . he's been touching me in a way I don't like . . . and I don't want him to.' Julia burst into tears again.

Her mum sat holding her. 'I'm glad you've told me. Why didn't you tell me before?'

Julia said, 'I didn't know how. I thought I'd be in trouble and that . . . you wouldn't love me any more.'

'Don't worry, Julia, I'm *not* angry with you. It's

not your fault. I only wish you had told me right away so I could have stopped it.'

Julia's mum thought for a minute. 'Maybe that's why you've been having all those bad dreams?'

Julia nodded, feeling safe for the first time in a long while.

'I was so afraid you wouldn't believe me,' said Julia.

'Of course I believe you. I know you wouldn't make up something like that.'

Julia gave her mum a big hug. Then her mum took her on her lap, just like she used to when she was a baby. Julia was so glad the secret was out.

'Mum?'

'Yes, Julia?'

'What's going to happen to Uncle Simon?'

'I'm not sure, Julia, but Dad and I will have to tell someone else about this. Uncle Simon has a problem and he needs help. Sometimes people who do this even have to go to prison, but we hope he'll have help so he can stop doing this to children. Whatever happens, *it isn't your fault*. He's the one with the problem and he shouldn't have done this.'

Julia got frightened again. Maybe she should say it wasn't true; that she had made it all up. Then she thought about Ben. It wasn't only her that this had happened to and maybe telling would stop it happening with Ben or someone else. What should she do about Ben? Knowing Ben, she didn't think he would ever tell. He was even more frightened than she was.

Julia asked to be alone for a while and her mum left.

Ben can't tell his mum, she thought. *Who can he tell?*

He had asked her not to tell anyone. What should she do?

Julia thought and thought. *I've got to tell and try to help Ben, as well.*

Feeling quite tearful, Julia went back into the kitchen again. 'Mum, there's something else . . .' She told her mother everything. Julia was feeling very tired.

'Would you like me to tell Dad or do you want to?' asked her mum.

'I'd rather you did, Mum. I'm so tired now.'

Julia said she didn't want anything to eat and she went to her room. She was reading when her mum and dad came in to say goodnight a little while later.

Mum must have told Dad, thought Julia. *He looks upset.*

'Julia, I'm glad you told Mum about what's been happening to you and to Ben. We've been talking and we want you to know that we will protect you and that you can talk to either of us whenever you feel like it.'

'Dad, before you do anything about Ben, can we talk about it?'

Her dad nodded. 'We'll try to let you help make some of the decisions in the next couple of days if you like, but some things we will have to do. We have to make sure that Ben is safe, too.'

Mum and Dad kissed her goodnight.

Julia felt so relieved. She found herself crying again, but this time it was because it was going to be all right. Julia fell asleep and didn't wake up till morning. She hadn't had any bad dreams.

CHAPTER THIRTEEN

Good Friends

When Julia got to school the next morning, Gill was waiting for her.

'Hello, Julia,' said Gill. 'How are things?'

'Fine, thanks.'

'I've been thinking about what you said . . .' began Gill.

'Gill, it really is all right. I talked with my friend and she told her mum. Both her mum and dad believed her and are helping her. So she's feeling good for the first time in ages.'

Gill looked closely at Julia. Julia did seem to be much happier. Gill felt certain that it had been Julia who had the secret. She also knew now that Julia had told and got help. But Julia had a right to her privacy and as long as she had help, Gill was happy. Gill decided she wouldn't ask Julia anything, but said:

'Julia, if you ever want to talk to anyone, you can talk to me.'

'Thanks, Gill.' Julia felt even better.

Mrs Simpson was waiting for the class when they all went in.

'Good morning,' she said, 'I have a secret to tell you today.'

'Is it a good secret?' said Charlie.

'Well, I think so,' replied Mrs Simpson. 'Some of you might have noticed that I've been getting a bit fatter lately. My secret is that I'm going to have another baby.'

Mrs Simpson had certainly kept that secret very well. No one had even suspected.

Mark thought of Nicky and wondered if Mrs Simpson knew what she was in for.

'Congratulations!' said Steven, who was very good at knowing the right thing to say.

Mrs Simpson thanked him.

Charlie thought it was a good excuse for not working, but Mrs Simpson didn't agree and they were soon busy.

At lunch Amy and Gill talked about the baby and how lucky it was to have a mother like Mrs Simpson.

'Her little girl is really lovely, maybe she'll have a boy this time,' said Gill, who had always wanted a brother.

'No way!' said Amy. 'I hope she has another girl. Sisters are better than brothers any day.' Besides all the animals in her house, Amy had three brothers. It was like living in a zoo sometimes.

'Maybe it will be twins,' said Julia who was sitting next to Gill.

'Wouldn't that be great!' said Gill. 'Listen, let's have a surprise party for Mrs Simpson and get her a present.'

'Yes, we could get Miss Parsons to keep her away while we decorated the room . . .'

'Some people could bring cakes and biscuits . . .'

'We could collect money from everyone . . .'

'If they could afford it,' said Amy. 'Maybe everyone could bring an envelope, so no one would be embarrassed.'

'Let's talk to the rest of the class, but tell them it has to be a secret or the surprise will be ruined.'

By the time they got outside, most of the class already knew and those that didn't soon found out. Charlie was threatened with instant death if he so much as dropped a hint about the party.

Mrs Simpson usually went to the staff room while they were in the library on Monday afternoon. If Miss Parsons made sure that Mrs Simpson didn't come back to the classroom, that would give them all of library time to set up. It would also give everyone time over the weekend to bake and get ready.

By the end of the day, they had all agreed to go home and ask if their parents could help and report back tomorrow to either Amy or Gill.

That afternoon, Gill walked home with Julia.

'You know,' said Julia, 'you were a big help to me.'

Gill was a bit embarrassed, but really pleased that Julia felt that way. 'I think kids can help each other sometimes, don't you?' she said.

'Yes,' replied Julia thoughtfully. She felt sure she was helping Ben, but she couldn't tell Gill that.

They walked for a distance without talking, but feeling very comfortable.

As Julia was turning towards her house, she

turned to Gill. 'Someday I'll tell you . . .' she started to say.

But Gill interrupted her. 'If you ever want to talk, just let me know. I'm glad you're all right now.'

They looked at each other and smiled. They both knew that they would be friends for a long time.

After saying goodbye to Julia, Gill walked home feeling good. She pushed the back door open. *Mum must be home*, she thought, *or it would be locked*.

'Mum, I'm back! What's for tea?' she said, throwing her books and jumper on the chair and heading for the kitchen.

'Well, you're certainly back to normal,' exclaimed her mother.

'Guess what happened at school today?'

'What?'

'Mrs Simpson told us that she was going to have another baby! We want to have a surprise party for her next Monday. Will you help?'

Then Gill smelled the most delicious smell in the whole world coming out of the oven.

'Scones! Great! When will they be ready?'

'Not so fast, young lady. One thing at a time. Help lay the table and let's talk.'

When Gill was getting out the plates, she told her mum about the party.

When everything was ready, they sat down. Her mum brought out the scones. 'Watch out, they're hot,' she warned, but too late. Gill reached for one and screeched as she burnt her fingers. 'Serves you right for being greedy,' said her mother.

'Sorry, Mum. Will you help with the party?'

'Yes, I'll help, but I want you to help me, too.'

'How?' asked Gill, with a mouthful of scone.

'Do you want to tell me why you were upset yesterday?'

Gill became quiet.

'Would you like to talk about it?'

'Well, it's sort of a secret,' said Gill.

'A good secret?'

'Not really . . .'

Gill's mum waited.

'I'll tell you, but I won't mention any names, all right?'

'All right.'

'A friend told me that a friend of hers had an uncle who had been hugging and kissing her.'

'A lot of uncles do that. Your uncle George gives everyone hugs and kisses.'

'But, Mum, this uncle said it had to be kept a secret. Besides, it wasn't nice kissing like Uncle George does. It made her feel uncomfortable and kind of frightened, especially having to keep it a secret. And . . . there was some touching she didn't like either.'

'Oh, I see, Gill,' said her mum. 'How did you find out about it?'

Gill told her mother what had happened.

'You were a very good friend and I'm glad that she told her mother,' said her mum. 'But what if her mum hadn't believed her. What would you have done then?'

'I would have told you or Mrs Simpson, but I thought it was better that she could tell someone she trusted herself.'

'Children can often help each other, just like you did. I'm sure that talking with you gave her the courage to tell. I'm proud of you for helping.'

Gill grinned and reached for another scone.

Gill's mother was quiet for a moment.

'Gill, you know that most adults try to protect and love children.'

Gill nodded and thought about Uncle George and the lovely toys be brought her. He was the best uncle in the whole world. Aunt Daphne was also a favourite because she always seemed interested in what Gill was doing.

'But what would *you* do if anyone ever asked you to keep a kiss, a hug or a touch a secret, or something like this happened to you?'

Gill knew she was lucky. She could tell her mum and her mum would believe her and help. Some kids might have to tell lots of people before someone believed them and that would be hard.

'I'd tell you or Dad or Gran or Aunt Daphne.'

'Good girl! Now let's clear up these dishes and you can get on with your homework.'

'Mum?' said Gill. 'You're great!'

CHAPTER FOURTEEN

It's Been a Good Year

It was the last day of school before the summer holidays. It had been a good year for the class. They agreed that Mrs Simpson had been their best teacher ever. The party they had planned had been a complete surprise and she had been really pleased. In the autumn they would be going forward to a new teacher, and would certainly miss Mrs Simpson; but she had said they could come back for a visit.

By then she would have her new baby.

Everyone had grown up so much this year and a lot had happened.

Mark hardly ever thought about the stranger any more, especially since the police had arrested him about three months after he approached Mark. Mark and all the children had learned what to do if anyone made them feel unsafe.

Deirdre hadn't had any more phone calls, but she was prepared and knew what to do if it happened again. She was glad they had talked about personal safety during the school year. It helped to know that other children had also had to deal with things like rude calls and flashers, and that she could share her fears with them and Mrs Simpson if she wanted to.

Julia was getting help from a counsellor and was talking to her mum a lot. She thought she would tell Gill someday how much having her as a friend had helped. But she wasn't ready to talk about it with her yet. She was still glad that the secret was out and these days she smiled more than ever before. Of course, the other children didn't know, but she didn't want them to. It was something private.

Her cousin Ben was having a difficult time talking about what had happened to him, but Julia hoped he would find it easier sometime soon. At least he was talking to her and that had helped them both. Right now that was all she could do. Uncle Simon was just beginning to admit that he had a problem. Maybe he would get better, as well.

Gill thought she might like to be a counsellor when she got older, because she liked helping people. She was looking forward to the holidays because she was going to stay with her Uncle George and Aunt Daphne. She knew, as did her mum, that she would be spoiled rotten and she couldn't wait.

All the children had learned about keeping safe and Mrs Simpson decided to go over again the things to remember, before saying goodbye for the summer. In fact, Mrs Simpson thought that personal safety was one of the most important lessons they had learned this year.

'Over the holidays, remember that we talked about how most adults love and protect children. But let's see if you remember what we learned to do if anyone asks you to keep touching a secret, or does something which makes you uncomfortable or confused.'

She wrote on the board.

**IF ANYONE MAKES YOU FEEL UNSAFE
YOU CAN:
SAY NO!
GET AWAY TO A SAFE PLACE!
TELL AN ADULT YOU TRUST!**

'And if someone doesn't believe you the first time you tell?' asked Mrs Simpson.

Everyone said together:

'KEEP TELLING UNTIL SOMEONE BELIEVES AND HELPS YOU!'

'Well done!'

Then she wrote on the board: XOXOXOXO

'What does that mean?' asked Amy.

'It's no secret that those are good hugs and kisses from me. I'll miss you all,' said Mrs Simpson. 'Have a lovely summer and come back safely next year.'

Where Children Can Get Help

The best way to get help is to talk to someone you know and trust, like your mother, father, stepmother or stepfather, grandparents, aunts, uncles, cousins or other relatives or family friends. Teachers, school nurses or your family doctor might also listen and help, though they cannot promise to keep what you say a secret. They may need to tell someone else to help you. Sometimes it helps to tell a friend and then go with the friend to an adult who can help.

But some children have no one they can talk to. If you feel that way or have a friend who needs help, you can ring one of these telephone numbers.

Telephone Helplines:

Childline 0800 1111
Kidscape 020 7730 3300
NSPCC Helpline 0800 800 5000
Samaritans 08457 909090
Children's Legal Centre 01206 873820

A selected list of titles available from Macmillan Children's Books

The prices shown below are correct at the time of going to press. However, Macmillan Publishers reserve the right to show new retail prices on covers which may differ from those previously advertised.

Michele Elliott
The Willow Street Kids
Be Smart, Stay Safe	0 330 35184 2	£3.99
Beat the Bullies	0 330 35185 0	£3.99

Celia Rees
The Bailey Game	0 330 39830 X	£4.99

All Pan Macmillan titles can be ordered from our website, www.panmacmillan.com, or from your local bookshop and are available by post from:

Bookpost
PO Box 29, Douglas, Isle of Man IM99 1BQ

Credit cards accepted. For details:
Telephone: 01624 836000
Fax: 01624 670923
E-mail: bookshop@enterprise.net
www.bookpost.co.uk

Free postage and packing in the UK.
Overseas customers: add £1 per book (paperback)
and £3 per book (hardback)